CHRONICLES OF THE TIME THIEF

(an autistic romance)

BOOK ONE

SONG OF EDEN

Richard Alan Poe

coincidental.

Chapters

Prologue

There are many well-written books available concerning the subject of autism. They range from well-meaning people offering advice from their own practical experience to a treasure trove of researched information on speculated therapies and treatments. I would advise you to read all of it. Knowing is power. Armed with that knowledge, you can affect a positive influence in your own life, or the life of another, who has been impacted by autism.

From inception, this series of books was intended to be a work of great importance to the ASD community. Beneath the fact and fiction of its pages lays a powerful message. It speaks equally of hope, defiance, and understanding while acknowledging the many contributions of the autistic individual, both past, and present.

By buying this series of books, and encouraging others to do so, you are providing the means and the chance to full fill a dream. A dream to improve the lives of others who live within the spectrum by providing a treatment program that recognizes and enhances the unique abilities associated with the autistic condition.

This story is about an autistic savant's desperate quest to save the woman he loves and the future of humankind.

The story is both entertaining and a satisfying read, pulling at the heartstrings of your emotions as it takes you on a grand adventure, leaving you laughing or crying all at the right and wrong moments. Here is joy, love, pain, and betrayal, carried by a mystery that

journeys through the fabric of time itself.

"I write so I can reach you." Richard Alan Poe

About the author

I am a diagnosed as a high functioning autistic, displaying a higher intelligence, while exhibiting savant like tendencies. I was born that way and have lived my life as an artist, playing multiple musical instruments, while exploring countless other forms of creative mediums. This has often left me hovering at the edge of fame at times, and having found I'm not always comfortable with that, I have therefore chosen as a writer the path of anonymity. My thinking being my critics would have a much harder time finding me. I have therefore taken the pen name of Richard Alan Poe. There is a family connection to the Poe family. My mother often repeated a story of those said relations, angrily burning any of Edgar Alan Poe's book they happened to come across. It seems he had made himself unpopular. Sorry, that's all I know. Poor maybe Uncle Edgar was likely an autistic too. His life reads like that.

I would truly like to thank you for your interest in my book. There will be seven books written in all, each episode building on the other, gaining strength, soaring towards a shockingly impossible to write climactic ending. However, if you have just bought my book, and are just now wondering what you have gotten yourself into, then in the name of the ASPERGIAN NATION (that's a website that helped me publish), bless you and all your family to come until the end of time eternal. The research I am involved in is important and the funds you have given will help to make that research possible.

I dedicate the CHRONICLES OF THE TIME THIIEF series to the women who most influenced my life, my wife Marie, my mother Thelma, and my mother in-law Jessie.

FOREWORD

Having a time machine opens up an endless world of possibilities. You can think for days on end and never really run out of new ideas to screw up. The first and most important thing to remember is not to tell anyone at all you have one. At this point, you may ask," Isn't writing about this basically doing just that?" Sheldon and I don't power this up till the May 30th in the year 2031 … so we're cool. It's not like you really believe me anyways and as long as the military thinks the same we can get away with no end of shit. The reason I know we invent a time machine, is because I told myself I did.

Chapter 1 - THE TIME THIEF

The sounds coming from the forest around me seemed anything but peaceful. The velvet stillness of night has always attracted me, but this was more. It was very much alive. The insects were very happy enjoying what was such a beautiful night, going about eating the foliage or each other. There were night birds with shrieks and calls to their bird friends, mostly saying "Hey, look at all those tasty bugs." It was a community.

I avoided Looking at the bright lights of the homes across the lake. It had taken me twenty minutes to adjust my eyes to see in the dark. A single glare of light would take that away from me. It was the harvest moon, and it filled the sky. The path through the forest was bathed in a silver light. One would expect a ferry or sprite to be crushed underfoot at any moment.

My favorite way of dog walking was to let the dog just go and I sort of come along. You never know where the two of you will end up. It was so light out tonight Prince had decided to lead me into the woods. He had been right about one thing. Everything really smelled great here. Right now, however, I was wondering if I had really thought this through. Predators here were rare but this was still their turf. Although I had never seen a bear or a cougar here ever I had brought my bear stick with me. One never knew. After all, I had brought my little big dog along. He was literally cougar bait on a string.

I pulled the belt of my robe tighter. I had gone Scotsmen, as I like to call it. Just a robe, mud boots, my trusty mega flashlight, and a stick from the garden was all I had with me. Prince was busy anointing yet another bush, relentlessly marking his territory. This was number eighty-seven tonight. I like to keep count. It always amazed me how much piss he could hold for such a little dog. Prince was a King Charles Cavalier Spaniel with all his bits. He works as my comfort dog. Leaving his balls on had caused a number of fights with other males who didn't have theirs anymore. It was the dog version of male penis envy. Having his working parts had given him no end of piss and vinegar and Prince wasn't above rubbing that in when he met up with other dogs. I found if I could get the dogs to sniff butt all would be well, either that or one of them would take off the others tail.

I loosely held his leash as he finally found a small bush to squat over. My dog was very polite about taking a dump. He always stepped away from a path or sidewalk, then hovered his anus over some offending foliage, to place his dung neatly onto it. Our whole neighborhood and the surrounding woods were full of his creations. What can I say, as an artist he was, prolific? It occurred to me, that should anyone meet with my displeasure, the two of us could redecorate their flower beds with festive little brown Christmas trees. A great horned owl called out from a branch above me.

"Who?" she cried.

I could see her up there spinning her head around, regarding us with rapt curiosity, perhaps considering if Prince would make a tasty meal. We like to call her Ellen.

"Who?" she cried again.

I was in no hurry to return home. The night was beautiful. I stopped still. There was the sound of snapping twigs from something large moving through the brush. Both Prince and I both dropped down in defensive mode. I with my stick and he with his threatening growl. The trees parted, and a large buck stood in the moonlight. I had encountered this animal before, but never this close up and personal. I stood still, facing him down, suddenly aware of all those pointed things on top of his head. He was magnificent. Prince gave a wolf-like snarl and lunged forward. The buck reared and bolted off, crashing through the brush. I got a good hold on Prince's leash and continued with our walk.

Home was but a few minutes away now. Hopefully, June and I could sleep well knowing there would be no accidents on a rug tonight. I had left my wife in bed, having slipped out quietly so as not to wake her. A whisper of music drifted through the trees. It became clearer gaining more resonance with each step I took. Our path now brought us to the most perilous part of our journey.

The trolls sat still, one for every tree or bush. Their grotesque eyes and mouth open and gaping, as if mocking us in our passage. The faint piano music echoing through the forest would have made this magical if they hadn't been so hideous. The woman who made them had placed them strategically to ward off any intrusion beyond the boundary she had set. These were her troll guards so to speak.

"Go back, for my property lies beyond"

This lady had a very sharp tongue and had earned the distinction as being known as the troll lady. I looked down to see Prince shitting on one of her minions at my feet. He didn't like the troll statues either. Funny how they looked a bit like her. I decided that her creation looked far better after Prince had got done with it, so I left it. How he managed to fill up the troll mouth was beyond me. I gave Prince a pat on the head and kept moving.

I emerged at the edge of my property to see the lights on in my studios. Someone was playing the grand piano. The flow and beauty of the notes were in a style not unlike my own, but much more advanced. It was, sublime.

I found him sitting at the piano. It wasn't hard to recognize him because he was me. Naturally, this was unsettling, to say the least. All kinds of early Twilight Zone episodes were flashing through my mind. Maybe I was dreaming this. Spellbound I watched as deftly he ran his fingers over the keys. In a flourish, he brought his piece to a climatic, and melodic ending.

"That was beautiful," I said. "Is it ours?" Oddly, this seemed like the right thing to say at that moment.

The me from 2033 rose to his feet.

"It's still unfinished." He replied "We call it, the song of Eden. You and I learned the melody from a good friend."

After an uncomfortable moment (I was still holding my bear stick) he smiled politely and asked me to follow him into the living room. Prince was there chewing at the foot of what looked like a Wurlitzer organ with a racing car seat strapped onto it. There was an imperceptible hum coming from it as if someone had left the power on. The older me didn't look all that much different. If anything he exuded an aura of peak physical condition. I figured maybe I had finally got around to using that gym membership I had. He explained that this was a result of the anti-aging research advancements I would put out in the 2020's. Prince looked up at the two of us, trying to work this out for a moment, then gave up. He sat down to beg for a doggy treat.

We laughed when we both took one out of our pocket and gave them to him. It was an icebreaker. The older me patted Prince's furry head and informed me that he still owned his Descendent King Charles the Fifth. Did you ever wonder if you ever met yourself would you even like you? When both of you have high functioning autism, it gets even more complicated. We worked it out. Apparently, the older me was on a mission. He and Sheldon had made it into NORAD in 2027 and unplugged their nukes, and now they had to lay low for a bit. I asked about his ride, and he let me get up on it. The leather seat seemed to fold around me as the control panel lit up like a jet fighter. Older me gave me a quick run through then flashed me a smile,

"There's a package under the seat. You might need that."

He punched the large red button. You know, the one you're never supposed to touch. The Wurlitzer rose to a threatening hum. The room started to spin, and my vision became a blur. Was that Prince leaping in to save me? Older me was shouting something,

"Sorry, I just wanted to have some time with my wife again! Don't worry; you'll be back in a week or so! Say hi to Lucy for me." All I could come up with was "Hey, what?" Everything went black

Chapter 2 - DEAR FURUCK

The darkness continued for a very long time until I began to realize that is exactly what it was. I was someplace very dark. Small sounds permeated the cold silence. Water was dripping somewhere edged with noises of something stirring. I had taken Prince out earlier for his walk and the mega flashlight I bought in shop smart was still in my pocket. I whipped it out and hit the high beam. The ceiling above me exploded in a frenzy of fleeing wings. I dropped down under the time machine and switched my light to a penlight size. I was sheltering from literally a shit storm of bat droppings. That's when I noticed the silver suitcase strapped there under the seat. I snatched the note taped on top and read it between breaths. This was because I was somewhere between a panic attack and heart failure. The note was in my own handwriting addressed to myself.

Dear me;

The very first thing to do is don't panic. I know that's coming a little late right now but think it through. I came to you from the year 2033 and I was all in one piece. So, you're fine right? Don't try jumping off a cliff or anything testing this but both you and Prince get back here totally all right so just calm down. The you in 2033 (me) packed you this case to keep you safe. The wife and I are off to Paris in the morning so don't worry, and there's just this one last thing, remember you can't change anything. Whatever happens, always happens; so don't beat yourself up about that when you shoot Bob.

I glanced around the tiny cave to get an idea of where I was. Small eyes blinked back at me from the corners then scurried away. Rats, I thought, or something like rats. This seemed like the ideal time to open my survivor suitcase. Right on top was the biggest shiniest handgun I'd ever seen. It was a weapon of the future. Each clip held a lot of high caliber rounds. Also in the case were a toothbrush, candy bars, and a bunch of things I'd have to go through later. I pulled out what looked like thin black long johns and quickly put them on. To my surprise, I was instantly warm. After strapping on my pistol I looked like some ninja who gets offed in a video game. Tossing my now useless clothing into the case I began searching for a way out. It took

some time but I located a small opening and

emerged into what appeared to be a much larger

section of the cave. The faintest emission of light

showed ahead of me leading me upward. I stopped

suddenly.

Terrible sounds were coming from that direction.

Women and children were screaming in terror.

Then, came the roar. It echoed down towards me in

the darkness. Fear is not something that autistics work well with. It was all I could do not to piss myself in my new ninja pants. Instead, I found myself running towards the sounds. I burst out into the larger part of the cave. An enormous dark shadow crouched in the cave's opening. It rose ready to pounce on what looked to be a young girl fallen before it. The only thing keeping it at bay was a small black and white dog gnashing his teeth at it.

Rushing in, I flicked on my mega beam and screamed, "Fuck off!" I know, kind of lame, but it was all I could think of. In the blinding light, stood a massive bear as big as an SUV, brandishing super-sized claws and teeth. The girl rolled away and grabbed a burning branch from a fire then jammed it into something that caused it to erupt like a volcano. Leaping through the air she stabbed it into the monster's face. Howling, it fled the cave, leaving the smell of burning fur. I became aware that I had been holding my gun, pointing it. I holstered it and got hold of Prince in order to calm him down. No need, he was absolutely elated. He leapt into my arms and showered me with doggy kisses. This was as much action as he had seen in his whole life. Poor thing just never seems to understand how little he really is. In his mind, he's a really big dog. The young girl was just standing there looking at us. I showed her a smile and came over to her. Sometimes having a dog designed to look like a cute puppy for its whole life has its perks. A companion dog can make it easier to interact with other people. Prince's real superpower was that he could win you over with one look of his big dark brown eyes. The girl reached out her hand, tentatively allowing Prince to lick her fingers. She giggled and we laughed together. Others in the cave came forward. There were two small boys. Identical twins I came to call Ugg and Glugg. Their mother, Uma appeared thin and old yet had the eyes of a woman in her 30s. All these people seemed happy to see me and after a few days in their company, I came to understand why. Lucy took me by the hand and showed some drawings at the back of the cave.

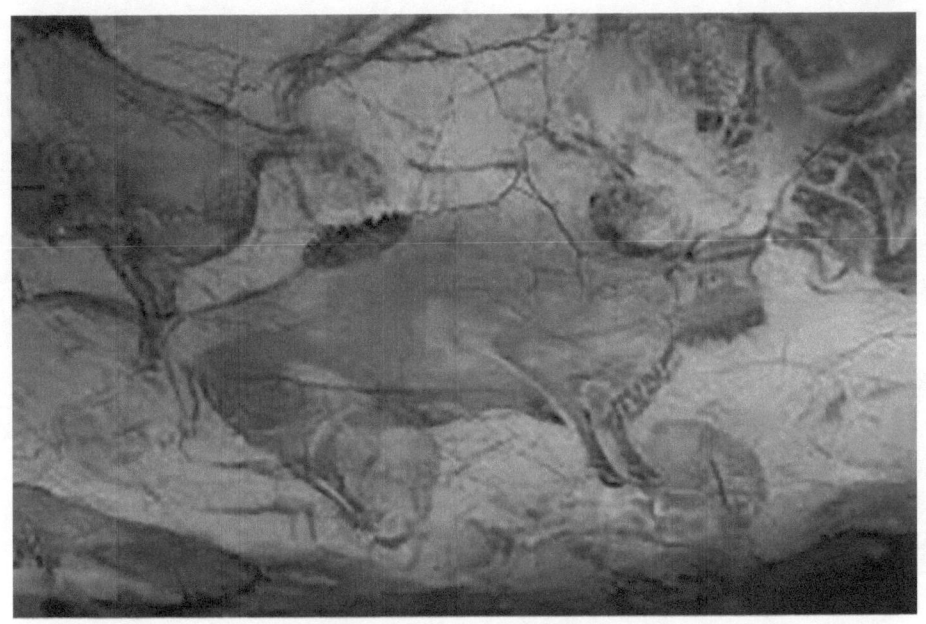

She again lit a branch dipped into the strange powder. In the glittering light, she pointed to two men running after a herd of woolly mammoths. Lucy demonstrated with a series of grunts and shrieks how this event ended with the men being stomped on.

She expresses this in tears on her hands and knees pounding her fist into the ground shrieking, "Thud, thud, thud!"

There were no men here now, no one to hunt for them, or protect them. They were all alone. Communication got easier when it finally occurred to me that all the gesturing and grunts they used was because everyone here thought I was stupid. Their language was limited to only a few words simply derived from the sounds around them. Drop a rock and it goes thud. Hit the rock with another rock and you get the word rock etc. The twins followed me everywhere, naturally curious about everything about me. Late at night Lucy and I would talk or least she did. Conversations to her consisted of her going on excitedly for endless periods without allowing anyone else a moment to speak. Naturally direct eye contact was fleeting. Once I had discovered I was on the spectrum I worked to correct this in myself. I scan the speaker's right eye studying them like a detective trying to analyze them. Autistics avoid eye contact for the simplest of reasons. We don't want to. Overcoming that can give you the edge in encounters with NT's. The other reason is, that after a while, each person you meet begins to look like someone you have met, over and over again. By looking straight and hard into someone's eyes, you see that person is uniquely themselves, and no one else. The eyes are the window to the soul. The answers you seek, are there. I reached out and held Lucy's face in my hands and looked into hers. She was an autistic female in the stone age. It was she who did the painting of the cave wall. The one who found a way to use the manganese dioxide as a fire started. A shock went through me. I knew why I was here now. Lucy was my ancestor.

One day Lucy drew out on the ground an image of herself and someone else holding hands, then, pointed longingly out of the cave into the valley below. Lucy, it seemed had a boyfriend somewhere out there. I smiled to show her I was happy for her and asked her his name. She placed her hands over her heart and she told me. His name was Bob.

THE EVOLUTIONARIES

At 49,261,083, autistics now represent the largest rising minority in history. More than ever, presenting a positive awareness for the autistic condition, is key to acceptance and understanding in our world. The general population must be allowed not to merely to see some one person who is different, but that they are a part of an entire people, representing a clear and distinct society. One where they and the people who support them can voice their concerns in all matters that ultimately affect their lives.

Man is now facing a mass climate change. One that is happening in our own time. The autistic Charles Darwin (yes, he was one too) would tell you that the speed of a species evolution will rise at a proportionate rate to the challenges of its environment. It remains that as our environment changes, so also must we. I often wonder if autism is not a disease, but an intricate part of the evolutionary process. That the reason Autism has continued to exits as an evolutionary trigger, is because it was needed.

Chapter 3 - WILD THINGS

In the cold of night my tribe, as I now thought of them, would snuggle down under a pile of animal furs and try to out snore each other. Between their warm bodies and all the farting, they seemed to find the warmth they needed to get them through. Naturally, Prince was in there somewhere. To him, this was doggy heaven.

I stood at the caves opening looking up into the heavens. There was no moon tonight and the stars shone brightly. The large comet, that had gained my interest, appeared closer with each night. It could be Halley's, but there was no way to know for sure. Following a highly eccentric trajectory around the Sun, comets have a long history, usually as omens and bearers of bad news. Made of rock and ice they may take hundreds, thousands or in some cases even millions of years to complete one orbit. The extinction event 65 million years ago is now widely believed to be the result of a

comet striking the earth. It killed off about 70% of all species on Earth, most notably the dinosaurs. The enormous collision would have triggered fires, earthquakes and huge tsunamis. The dust and gas thrown up into the atmosphere would have depressed global temperatures for several years.

When I was sure everyone was sound asleep, I took a moment to go down into the cave to checkup on my time machine. I was a little worried about the rats eating the wiring, but no worries, there was no wiring. However, this thing was put together, or whatever powered it, was way beyond my understanding. In fact, there wasn't even a speck of dust or bat carp on it. I trained the beam of my light on the cave's ceiling. There were no bats. I surmised that the machine was putting out some kind of powerful wave, one that the bats couldn't navigate through. That's why they had all gone.

The contents of my silver survivor suitcase revealed an endless treasure of "God I need that!" My warm ninja-like suit came with some mass upgrades. It was, as I thought, military grade. This was confirmed by the red tag pinned to it stating, military surplus final sale; no returns. Apparently, it had been on markdown. Space like boots, gloves with strange buttons, a belt with a big red button on it, everything I could want for Christmas. I suited up, pulled up my hoody, and went looking for a mirror.

My mega light illuminated the dark pool. Was this really me in the reflection, a kind of cyber-ninja from the future with poor fashion sense looking back?

I laughed then stopped suddenly. I remembered the gun. The presence of the gun bothered me. Was I, in the future, running from something? What was that he said, something about NORAD? Is this why he had this defensive like suit? I tried to shake it off.

The last part of the suit was a heavy pair of what appeared to be dark sunglasses. I slipped them on. After all, everything is cooler when you're wearing shades, right? Translucent view screens flashed up showing statistical readouts. The cave bloomed into night vision. It was the voice that brought me to my knees. It was her voice.

"My name is June. How may I assist you?"

I spent the night with her, or at least a digital representation of her. It comforted me but I knew it wasn't real. The futuristic operating platform the glasses used seemed to know what I needed before I did. June gave an overview of the substance the suit was made of. What appeared to be simple cloth was really a type of composite bio nanotechnology. The suit was alive and it would do anything to keep itself that way. I was just getting comfortable with this when it stung me for the first time. For a moment I thought I had sat on a bee, or worse one had got inside the suit. June giggled and explained I needed a continuous course of meds to protect myself from getting sick. The suit was simply immunizing me against literally everything. Still, I wasn't going to be able to sit for a while.

June told me to "Suck it up ya big baby." then came up with a novel idea, "It's early yet. Why don't you go out for a walk? Take Prince with you. He's smelling up the cave anyways."

I wouldn't know, the overpowering stench I had found myself in had caused me to go nose blind day one.

Morning came over the distant snow-covered hills, giving light to the sparse greenery of the valley. The day showed the promise of a clear sky with the hint of warmth. Prince and I slipped quietly out of the entrance of the cave. I looked back to see if anyone had noticed. They were all there, smiling happily, lined up behind me. Food had gone scarce in the cave and it was market day. Lucy handed me a fur mantel to cover myself up with and a heavy club. Someone had taken a vote and I was to be the alpha male. I led them down into the valley.

We paused at the edge of a woodland and drank at a small stream. Lucy, like the others, moved silently. Each was constantly aware of their surroundings. The sounds of life were all around us. You were either predator or prey here. Ugg and Glugg went to work, gathering firewood for their mother. Every once in a while they would reach down and snatch something, be it from foliage or dirt, and popped that into their mouths. Lucky pulled up some kind of root and placed it into my hand, and swear to God said, "Yum" then motioned me to eat. I was absolutely starving. Deftly I knocked the dirt off of it, jammed it into my mouth, and chewed. I was somewhere between a radish and a turnip. When I attempted to help Lucy look for more she stopped me, pointed two fingers at my eyes, then waved her hand around her. You keep watch, she was saying.

We ate as we went along until we reached an area of open grassland surrounded by low trees. The boys climbed up into the trees to gather eggs. Prince was in hunting mode with his nose to the ground. I have had a number of dogs in my life but despite his size, Prince was a born hunter. Naturally, the animal scents here were driving him nuts.

We began laying out our spoils on a skin so we could tote them home. It was our grocery bag in this Garden of Eden. Lucy brought me a cute little mammal she had dragged out of a hole, and then happily snapped its neck. Prince spoiled the moment. It seemed he had found something of interest out there.

We came upon the largest pile of dung I had ever seen. Prince sniffed at it. Whatever had made this even he didn't want a piece of. The fact that it was so fresh it was literally steaming made this worse. Lucy caught her breath and looked around widely. Prince gave a low growl toward the tall grass. It seemed to be parting like a sea that was rushing towards us. The ground began to shake.

Lucy sounded the alarm, "Thud, thud, thud, thud, thud, thud!" then she ran for the trees. Prince had the good sense to follow. It was too late for me. I caught the flash of the rhino's horns as it bore down on me. Digging my heels into the ground, I turned to face him and pressed the red button on my belt.

There was a sharp pain as if I stuck my finger in a light socket. I phased out of time just as the beast lifted its deadly horns into my nuts. It was so quiet for a moment, so peaceful, and then I was back. The rhino had traveled right through me. Mindlessly, it carried on towards the remaining targets fleeing before it. Lucy had gained the trees and was ascending up into its branches. Prince, however, couldn't outrun the thing chasing him, and in no way could he climb a tree. He dodged hard to the right beneath the monster's feet. Swinging round his pursuer lumbered after him. I bolted forward at an unbelievable speed, scooped Prince up, and leaped upwards.

I remembered thinking, "Is this what it's like to fly?"

I took hold of the highest branch of the tree then looked down. My tribe in the lower limbs had forgotten about our aggressor and were staring transfixed up at us. They were as the Brits say, Gob smacked. The frustrated rhino was snorting and spinning in circles.

It might have simply gone away, all be it mad on its own, if not for the twins. Unsatisfied with just flinging down bits of branches, they pulled out their emerging manhood and proceeded to gleefully piss on him. This action only served to enrage the creature to the point of madness. He trundled off then tuned and lowered his horns towards us.

Bull-like his hooves raked the ground. He came on with all his fury. His charge struck the trunk of the tree with the force of a mac truck. The tree lost. Only a few remaining roots kept it from falling completely. The tribe survived the shock but not me. The branch I had hold of gave a loud snapping sound. The rhino looked up hopefully. Prince and I plummeted down like a stone.

I always aspired to be a surfer. The one and only time I tried I fell off my board in a mere heartbeat. I never truly recovered from that Hawaiian dude making fun of me when I lost the speedo I was wearing. Imagine my extreme surprise to break our fall by landing feet first on a great wooly rhino. Really, a pro gymnast couldn't have stuck it better. The rhino freaks out. In all my adventures this is one of my favorite moments. Prince and I, the wind in our faces surfing on the back of a terrified brute, racing through the high grass, might be at top of my list. It only lasted

36 seconds. My ride tumbled down under me rolling in a cloud of dirt and rhino snot. I whirled through the air tearing into the earth. Prince fell out of the sky like a football right into my arms.

I went to look at the rhino slumped on the ground. He didn't seem to be hurt in any way. He was just out of breath, and very much afraid. I looked into his eyes, patted him gently on the head, and went back to my tribe.

Chapter 4 – SNOWFLAKES

A lite snow had just begun to fall. I could make out the warm glow of our caves entrance in the fading light. It's funny how I have struggled in my life to be accepted by others. Yet here; so far from the life I had lived, was a home and a people that cared about me.

It was Prince who first picked up on the two sets of footprints in the snow leading into the cave. Uma had come back earlier with the intention of tending to the fire. Apparently, she had not come back alone.

The young man sitting by the fire with her came to his feet. He had a powerful and sturdy build with a dashingly rugged face framed by a mane of thick reddish blond hair, but the thing that really truly stood out about him was that he was not entirely human.

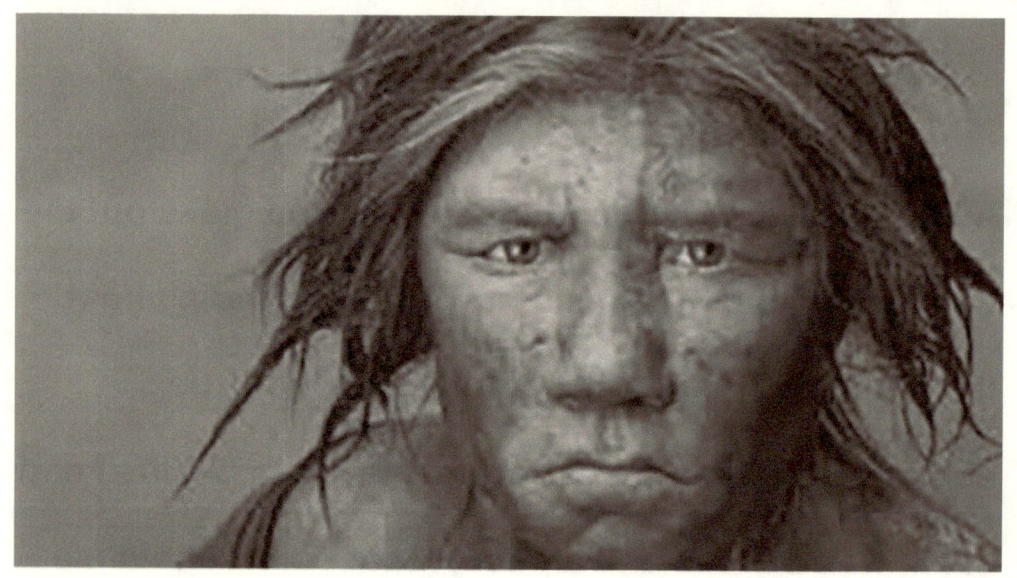

His boyish Neanderthal face came up in a tentative grin. Opening his arms wide he showed me his empty hands. Everyone was looking at me as if I should be doing something. Autistics really suck at understanding social cues and this was very much that moment. Uma sighed, came over and took the club out of my hands, carefully laying it down on the ground in front of me, then, she kicked me hard in the shins. Scolding me, she prodded me forward. I wasn't doing this right.

I mean you no harm. I needed to say, and I needed to say it soon, or else this was going to end badly. I showed him my empty hands and all of my teeth. I greeted him formally.

"You must be Bob?"

There was a general sigh of relief. Bob stepped up to me, chest to chest. Pressing his broad forehead against mine he looked hard into my face, taking the full measure of me. There was something there in his bluish grey eyes that held me, something that was again strangely familiar. His smile widened. The hug that came next nearly split my spine. Pandemonium broke out as he lifted me off my feet, carrying me as if I were a brand new toy. Everyone was slapping us both on the shoulders. When at last he put me down, he tapped his chest excitedly and said, "Bob" then tapped mine. He wanted to know my name. Before I could respond the tribe shouted out the name they had unfortunately given me that first night.

"Phruckoft" they chanted honoring me "Phruckoft, Phruckoft," their voices resounded through the cave. I had stopped a two-ton bear in his tracks with just two words of profanity. I suppose that would leave a lasting impression. Bob too was impressed and did his best to enunciate it. Strangely, his came close to the original, only he shortened it to Furuck. The name stuck.

When I grew up we were so misinformed about our evolution most of us thought we hung around with dinosaurs. More educated people knew that wasn't so but despite all their accumulative knowledge they still didn't have a clear understanding of how we all got to be the way we are now. Some years ago some very clever researchers linked our DNA to some

Neanderthal bones and found out most of us today are related to the fine specimen I saw before me. Remember that thick chested burly guy with the broad forehead and wide nose in gym class. The occipital bun was a knot of round bone located at the back of a Neanderthals skull for the attachment of their massive neck and jaw muscles. Feel at the back of your own head if you dare, there just below the occipital bone, is there a triangle? The traces of Neanderthal can be seen all around you. You just have to look. Order up a DNA report from any ancestry site and you'll see your amount of primitive listed there at the bottom. A lot of people in lower regions of Africa, however, test zero, as do many Afro Americans. Their ancestors didn't get up far enough North to get it on with the Neanderthal living there so they sort of got left out. The interesting thought here is that humankind is still continuing to evolve. We are ever changing ever mixing, then as now, perfecting what we are as a life form.

Needless to say, everyone here was happy to see Bob. It wasn't very hard to like him. Saying Lucy was happy just doesn't cut it. She was over the moon. With the niceties over, she threw herself into Bob with all the passion that a teenage girl can hold for a long overdue lover. All the smooching and heavy petting quickly gave way to more urgent needs. The two of them made their way back through the cave, momentarily lost in a world of their own.

Uma and the twins went about preparing what I like to recall was our Christmas dinner. Occasionally one of us would steal a glance back towards the two lovers. It was hard not to. They were both putting on quite a show. Both were in the peak physical condition of their lives. The musculature of their bodies was amazing to behold. Two coiled snakes, tightly entwined, intent in trying to devour one another does come to mind. Honestly, I found it truly beautiful. This was an expression of love shared between two people. Their union would perhaps produce an offspring, someone new to carry on their combined genetics in their bid to shape the future of humanity.

Dinner was somewhere between snacks with something like a potluck stew. Cooking was accomplished by whatever means possible using whatever was at hand to do it with. There were two massive bones that Bob had brought with him near the fire. Prince had been gnawing at these since we had got back. Uma pushed him aside, and bashed an opening into the bone, exposing the marrow.

Selecting a number of roots and what looked like withered fruit she stuffed the bones and laid them neatly onto the fire. This would be the main course as well as serve for a cooking stove and range. When the coals were hot enough, rolls of wet hide containing meat stripped from the small mammal, and a lot of things that would make a Billy goat puke were placed on the bone like grill to steam.

The noise at the back was beginning to piss Uma off. Lucy was shouting out, "Oh Bob, oh Bob!" A little too much for her liking. She picked up my club and went back to give them a hard poke and a couple of sharp words. She came back to the fire still muttering under her breath. The translation of which would come out as "Ass holes," in any language.

Eventually, the smell of a hot cooked meal brought everyone to take a place by the fire. There was an assortment of edibles laid out on a skin. Spotting the nummy radish-like roots, I reach out to select one. A sharp warning from Lucy made me take my hand back. There was a respectful silence, then. Uma led us all to join hands. She spoke softly as all lifted their eyes upwards. The words were few but full of meaning. She was giving thanks for all who were here and what we had together. After every person's name was mentioned all lifted their hands imploring the heavens.

"Aha!" they spoke into the darkness. These people had it seemed a belief, perhaps in some greater power which had a role in their existence, affecting the mystery of the world around them.

"All." I repeated after them. Uma smiled and handed me my radish.

All the food smelled good but surprisingly tasted even better. I couldn't get enough of the roasted slugs in the stew. When it came for the main course Ugg and Glugg took turns smashing the giant bones with my club. Each person was then given a portion in accordance to their place in the tribe. Bob as our guest and I as the respected leader were given the largest. The two of us scooped out some of the marrow stuffing it into mouths. The sublime taste nearly made us fall backward onto the cave floor. Sweet salty crunchy it was all there. Truly I had no words to describe it. Desert was withered fruit and nuts. Prince, as a descendant of royal dogs, had perfected begging to an art. All he had to do is turn his sad brown eyes on you and he could get anything from you. Finally, even he could eat no more. He lay down to pass out and fart by the fire.

Bob gestured to Prince and me, imploring Lucy to tell him about the two of us. Naturally, he was curious about how we came to be here. She got to her feet and motioned everyone to be quiet. The twins looked like they were going to pop with excitement. Between limited words, shrieks, and a lot of expressive movement she began enacted the events leading up to the present. Lucy turned out to be a master storyteller, sweeping us up in her primitive narrative. All gasped as she acted out the fending off of the bear, ending with her heroic trust with the flaming branch into its face. When the clapping stopped she began again. When it got to the part about Prince and I riding the rhino Bob's mouth dropped opened. This ended with Lucy riding Ugg as the rhino and poor Prince being snatched off the floor to be thrown about through the air, as the three of them were traversing across the cave floor. I expected Prince to puke at any moment.

To my knowledge, no one I know has ever heard a Neanderthal laugh. It is a rare privilege. The first thing is it comes in a higher pitch, permeated with uncontrollable gasps and snorts. The second thing is you may never ever get him to stop. After an hour even Lucy was getting concerned. Finally, Bob wiped the tears from his eyes, attempting to pull himself together, then took one look at me and start right in again. It came to a point someone had to do something.

Lucy started to clap her hands together. Following her lead, the twins began slapping some bones together, catching her rhythm. "U-U-U-u-m-m-m-mmmmmmm-o-o-o-h-h-h" she sang.

Everyone joined in the chant, "UUUUMMMMMMMMMOOOHHH". Bob rose to his feet and moved to stand at the cave entrance. Lit by the background of moonlight, stars, and the newly fallen snow he appeared to glow beneath an angelic light. There he stopped, as if gathering all the world around him. I knew what he was going to do, because I too, have done this. Turning slowly toward us he opened his mouth. That is when I heard him sing. It was so soft. One had to listen very carefully just to hear it. Rising through the chant and the rhythm his voice began to claim its place, striking out in a near-perfect pitch. The only way it could be described is that of a choir boy in an empty cathedral. His song hung in the air echoing seemingly without end, reaching down into my soul to touch me with its melody. This was the voice of my ancestors.

I would never forget it.

Later, when all were asleep, I went down to my small cave to look for my visor. It had been a wonderful night but I needed to talk to her. June, as always, was there waiting for me. Her image filled the screen.

"Merry Christmas," she said.

That night I took the gun and I hid it in a place I'd never be able to find it again.

Chapter 5 - THE HUNTING PARTY

In the next couple of days, Bob and I had become the best friends. For someone who barely ever said a word, Bob it had turned out, was quite the conversationalist. He could easily convey his intentions with a simple gesture or even a look. His people were few and lived a distance away near the edge of a river. There was enough fish as he told it for a man to walk on the water there, where one only had to reach into a puddle for your dinner. His real passion was for hunting large game. It was something that he was born for after all. The Neanderthal people had existed for over 250 thousand years through some of the toughest climates our world has ever seen. They had been quite successful until the homo sapiens arrived. The Neanderthal would then disappear in less than 10 thousand years. Their remaining genetics, found among us today, points to the fact that they were simply absorbed.

The paintings on the cave wall served as a power point presentation for Bob's exploits. He made the most of it often going on for hours about his many adventures. The bigger the beast the better was the way he saw it. In the time I had once lived it translated to the greater the risk the greater the gain. At rare times he was decently honest, shaking his head regrettably at his mishaps and failures, and that legendary one that had got away.

The twins had returned from foraging with a present for me. Two rows of dry tree branches layout on the cave floor. Bob went through them critically, picking out the ones that made his approval, then, solemnly presented me with two. One was long and very straight while the shorter one was of a sturdy thickness. I accepted them gratefully. The boys beamed happily. Instructing us to build a large fire Bob began setting out the items we would need. It appeared the three of us were to receive a lesson in the manly art of spear making.

When all were suitably seated our class began. Bob took a large hollow bone and began stuffing it with paper-like strips of bark from an ash tree. This done, with the use of a small rock and some wet clay, he sealed one end. The other end was more difficult to fashion due to the allowance of a tiny opening that was intended to be left there. He solved this with a split bird bone and more clay. Using larger rocks, he carefully made a range, then, propped up his creation with the end with the drain hole slanted downward. An upturned human skull placed at its lower end would serve as a collector for the oil this device would produce. I thought about asking about the skull, then, decided against it. I was better off not knowing. Adding coals from the fire Bob slowly built up the heat beneath his still. With the extraction process underway, he inspected the rocks we were to fashion into spearheads. We were to make two. The longer spear, a javelin for deeper penetration, would need to be smaller and more pointed while the shorted killing spear was to have a larger blade with a wider cutting edge.

Flint knapping is where you strike a weaker rock

with a hammer like stone that will shatter the weaker

stone hopefully into a useful cutting edge. Bob was an experienced expert in this. Turning his target stone deftly in his hands he removed flake after flake until the shape of a spearhead took shape. If at any point the quality of his work was at question he would toss it aside and start again. When he had one completed that was worthy of his attempt he dulled the edges with a piece of deer antler then began carefully applying softer strikes in order to bring out a more uniformed blade. A stone with a grittier surface was then used to sand down the blade to razor sharpness. All that was left was to do was add notches towards the hilt so that it could be affixed to the shaft of the spear. What Bob had accomplished in mere minutes took us countless hours. I am someone that enjoys shaping things with his hands and with considerable effort my finished work met the approval of my master. We knew the still was doing its work from the turpentine smell from the oil it was producing. Notching each shaft to fit perfectly to each spear tip was a matter of burning and chiseling and doing it again if you split your wood. Satisfied enough oil had been produced Bob added in some of the charred ash bark back in and brought this to a low boil. When the pitch had cooled slightly he rolled a smear onto to his finger testing it for tackiness. He grinned happily. Our glue was ready. We had spent a whole day prepping but now it was time to put this all together. Using strips of tough sinew, and the reheated glue, attaching the spearheads was completed in a matter of minutes. We were armed. Proudly all of us pranced about, jabbing and thrusting, acting out in mock battles with our weapons.

It was only a matter of time before one of us opened a vein or stuck someone else in the foot. Uma put a stop to this foolishness. We four had been making a mess for long enough and she needed to start dinner.

After we had eaten the four of us retreated to the rear of the cave where we could have some peace. It was our man cave within a cave. In the light of our fire, Bob and I talked about the day ahead. It was to be a great hunt, a hunt to be remembered by all. The boys had listened for a while but then nodded off to sleep, each with their new spears in their hands. We were to leave before dawn, and I too was ready for sleep. I asked my friend what game we were to pursue, thinking he would say deer. He raised his spear into the darkness to tap on the cave painting behind him, the one with the herd of mammoths. I caught my breath.

"Thud thud!" he said, then closed his eyes and fell instantly to sleep.

Chapter 6 - THE MAJESTIC

We left in cold darkness. By the time we had gained the edge of the woodlands, the stars had faded before the advancing light. I had left Prince behind. He might get in the way where we were going. That, or maybe he might get hurt somehow. The lite frost beneath our feet soon disappeared, and the chill that held the land gave way to the warmth of the day. Bob led us along a small river following what appeared to be a worn path. Footprints in the wet earth showed that others had traveled this way just recently. There were four sets of tracks Bob pointed out and he bid us to hasten our pace.

The river opened up to a wide shallow area offering a ford where we could cross. Resting upon the other bank sat the party we had been following. Bob waved excitedly to them and they greeted him cheerfully in kind. These were friends of his who he had hunted with many times. After exchanging bone-crunching hugs and all of the customary introductions, our troop moved out. We were now a party of eight.

The stocky older man was very much fully Neanderthal while the remaining three, possibly his sons, carried some of the same characteristics, but appeared mostly homo sapiens. My friend Bob was, I now realized, a product of encounters of repeated mixed relationship. We left the river, traveling into a wide grassland that swept away to a ridge of snow covered mountains.

Animal trace was everywhere. Finding spore was as easy as putting your foot down. The question was how fresh it was and what kind of creature it came from. The old man bent down over a clear set of enormous feline tracks.

He made the gesture of a clawed paw lashing forward.

"Katt!" he hissed vehemently.

Following his lead, we dropped down then crawled up a low rise. Here we were able to survey the surroundings below us. Many animals great and small skirted the edge of a large watering hole. It almost looked peaceful until you noted the small groups of carnivores stocking them.

Our prey moved majestically among them, their massive tusks assuring them their right of passage. The mammoth to the front, the matriarch, led the younger females and cafes, while a great bull guarded her flank.

A younger male, constantly looking behind it, covered the rear of the procession.

The others in my party saw the signs before I did. Bob pointed to the tall grass surrounding the water. Something was moving over there and stocking the mammoths. The opportunity came when one of the baby mammoths veered away from its mother to approach the water.

The saber tooth's sprung, rushing towards it. The bull wheeled, charged into them to cut them off. A wide swing of his tusk sent one spinning into the air.

Getting between them and the crying infant he lifted his great trunk, bellowed his rage.

There were three of them. They had the advantage. The big cats began to circle looking for an opening. They came at him from each side. Stamping his feet and heaving his tusk, the bull looked for a time to be able to drive them off, until one leapt up to open his neck with his long yellow teeth. The bull spun flinging off his attacker into the dusk. A bright spray of blood showed the depth of the bulls wound. It was then that his third enemy leapt up from behind him, clawing up his back.

The saber tooth opened his mouth to puncher the bull through the back of the head. This was how they killed. The young bull rushed in. Using its mighty trunk, it hurled the Saber tooth into the ground beneath their feet. Both of the mammoths began stomping it until it was nothing but a red smear in the grass. By then it was too late for the baby. The other two sabers had quickly made their kill. Now they were only keeping at a distance, waiting to feed. Other predators, hyenas, and jackals were gathering, also hovering at the edge of the feast.

The old bull sniffed the dead offspring for a moment then moved off to rejoin the herd.

There was nothing more he could do here. I had been a witness to nature at its most cruel, where the old the weak and the young were the first ones chosen to die. The fact remains, all that lives does so by consuming other life, and that includes both you and I.

The wound was mortal. Blood continued to flow freely from the wound on the old bull's neck. At the point he began fall back from the rest of his herd, Bob gave the sign for our troop to move silently forward. It didn't take long before the bull became aware of us. I knew this because he turned off in another direction, moving rapidly away from his family.

We were forced to break into a run. Our quarry was outdistancing us. Although the land rose steadily I did not slow my pace. Something was making me stronger. I felt as if I could run like this forever. I knew it wasn't because of the suit because I hadn't worn it. It was a risk, I knew, but I wanted this day to be real for me. Autistics desire to be accepted by others. I just wanted to be like everyone else, only I wasn't. I stopped to look back to see the others far behind me. Reaching for the pouch on my waist I took out one of the small dense chocolate bars that I had been nibbling on since I came here. I took a small bite and placed it under my tongue. The dark mixture began to expand. A strange sensation swept through me, confirming what I already knew. It was changing me, making me faster stronger. I returned to the hunt, bounded up the ever-rising landscape until I reached a small plateau. In the end, the trail of blood led me straight to him. The old bull was there waiting for me. There was nowhere left for him to run.

The two us stared at each other. We were only a few meters apart. I still had my spears with me but I had no wish to harm him. If he had any strength left in him, I knew he would still try to kill me, but he was too weak. I heard the shouts from the others behind me and then I saw him stumble. He fell backward tumbling over the edge of the plateau.

Finding the body of the mammoth was easy. The place where it had come to rest was marked by the scores of vultures circling overhead. It would take some time to make our way down to it.

I had gained considerable respect from the others. Alone I had run down and killed a large male mammoth in his prime, or at least that's the way Bob was telling it. I knew different. Wow, I thought, fake news was invented way back in the Stone Age. I guess we can all blame Bob for that.

When at last we had reached the spot we were miffed to find that a larger group of hunters had already moved in on our kill. They too had seen the vultures. I had faced many things this day, but this was the first time I had truly experienced real fear. These were fierce men. Their faces were painted, denoting their warlike allegiance to their equally warlike tribe. A large strong man brandishing a heavy stone axe stood planted before the mammoth, barring our way. A look from Bob told me showing them my empty hands here would only show our weakness. The old man stepped forward to reason with their leader. Pointing to me, he was explaining how I, Furuck, had ran down this mighty beast alone and had driven it off the cliffs to where it now lay. He explained that having achieved such a feat I had the right to claim this kill. He offered that here was enough for all and as they were many and we but few they may be allowed an equal share. The leader laughed cruelly, then, spit straight into the old man's face. Most people with autism have been at this place in their lives. The difference here is most bullies we face off against aren't armed with an axe threatening to split your head open. Autistics don't have the social skill to talk their way out of a violent confrontation. We only know fight or flight. Worse is how I personally have learned to deal with fear. I replace it with a blinding rage and the ability to defend myself. Striding straight up to the man I wrenched his axe out of his hands. "Furuck off!" I screamed threateningly. For a brief moment, everyone was stunned, then, the strong man gathered himself. Silently he raised his arm, pointed his finger at me. Every weapon was raised towards me. They were going to strike me down. Maybe I hadn't thought this through. It was at that very moment the mountain behind them raised itself. The mighty bull yet lived. It's battered and broken body writhed, caught in the finale throws of its own death. A tusk appeared rammed through the leader's chest, then whisked him away. The others close to him were trampled or crushed in a whirling cloud of blood and dirt. Claiming his enemies lives with him in death, the great Mammoth fell for the last time. All those that remained looked on in both amazement and unbelieving horror. It took a while for what had just happened to sink in. The leader of a mighty tribe and all his closest supporters had just been erased. From the look of the people around me, no one seemed to be very upset with this. It was the old man who spoke my name first. "Furuck" he said, raising his spear. The others, regardless of their tribe, followed him in this.

"Furuck" they shouted, raising their spears in salute to me. To them, I was now Furuck the Brave,

Furuck the Mighty Hunter. I added to their admiration by instructing them to attend to the wounded, then by bidding each man to take an equal share of the mammoth's flesh. All would go home to feed their people tonight. As my share, I took the stone axe for myself.

Chapter 7 – THE CALLING

I am a good dog. Everyone tells me so. Da Da had told me to stay, then he and the other males had gone away. He made it clear with his intentions that he would return so, I did as Da Da asked. I trusted him, and I had remained here, waiting for him and the other males to come back. Still, I worried. I was not there to protect them and to guide them home. Their scent was still strong here, in this big hole in the ground, but I could no longer find their smell on the wind. It had been dark then light many times now, and still, my pack had not returned. Soon it would be too late to follow them. Sometimes I would lay just outside the big hole in the ground, my head resting on my paws, staring into the distance, listening for a sign of their return.

I could sense the alpha females were worried too. They both got to be alpha because trying to determine who was dominate shifted from moment to moment. The older bent one spoke to me harshly, and I learned soon enough to stay out of the reach of the big stick she always kept close. The quick one, Lucy, was kindly and would sit with me for long periods of time, stroking my fur. Her voice was soothing, and she never seemed to stop talking to me. I liked that. Sometimes she would even rub my tummy. June used to do that for me, but I don't see her anymore. I think maybe she's still at the house on the lake, waiting for Da Da and me to come home. I think I love Lucy as I loved her. At night she would let me sleep beside her under the warm skins. The animals the skins belonged to weren't here anymore, so they didn't need their fur anymore. I had some idea what became of them, after all, I was lying on what was left of them, but I try not to think about it. My brain so I can't hold onto a thought too long anyways. Maybe someday my skin will end up here too.

The old bent female, the one called Uma, came out of our big den to sit beside me. I wagged my tail, hoping she would notice that I was a good dog too. I think maybe she is afraid of me. Slowly, she reached out her hand and patted my head, and then she also looked out toward the vast wilderness below us. She looked for a very long time, but like me, did not find the ones she sought.

I got up, moving to place my head in her lap, then looked up at with her my big brown eyes. Understanding those who need comfort is what I did best. The old woman was worried too. We sat there for a long time, sharing our pain.

That night, as in every night, the two females built up the fire near the opening. Above, I could see the twinkly lights and a part of the yellow ball that moved a crossed the sky. I was doing my job, watching and listening, guarding us against attack. This was something I could do better than the rest of my pack. At times, strange scents would come to me. There were other animals out there, prowling or hiding in the darkness. Unlike me, they had a fear of the fire, and mostly, that kept them away, but not always.

I pricked up my ears, listening for the sound that had come the night before, and the one before that. It had been long and wailing, forlorn in its sadness. She was lonely. If in fact, it was a she. It came now, closer this time than the night before. It struck me in my heart, then stopped, as if waiting for an answer from one of her own. None came. What kind of dog this was, puzzled me? There was no mistaking that it was likely large and fierce. Fear and curiosity raced through me. The howling came again, only this time it carried on the edge of pain. It was more than loneliness. It was a plaintive and desperate call for help.

Venturing to the furthest reach of the light of our fire, I sat back on haunches and lifted my face towards the yellow ball above. She was calling me, and I knew I must answer. Drawing all the air I could, I filled my lungs. Fearfully, I began howled back. The sound that came out of me was more like a weak and pathetic whine. I tried again, pushing out all of my air, only to achieve a spiral of unbalanced and disconnected notes. Clearly didn't have much of a singing voice. Moments passed. I was about to return to the safety of the fire when I heard the cry again. It was closer now, coming no longer from the hills, but from somewhere just below us. Whatever was making that sound, was making its way towards me. I began backing away, wary of the encounter. The scent of her reached me. There was the taint of fresh blood. Instinctively, the hair on the back of my neck began to rise. Out there beyond the flickering light of our fire, I felt her quietly watching me. Perhaps she was as curious about me as I was with her. She came, moved without sound. A dark shadow appeared. Bright glowing eyes burned into me, surrounded by a mysterious and massive shape.

I could feel her every breath on the biting cold, and

hear the beating of her heart. Transfixed, I looked

deep into her soul, and I found her there, looking

fiercely back into mine. My sense of self-preservation

kicked in. I brought my face into an intense growl,

baring my teeth. My growl osculated into a

threatening bark, warning her back. I wasn't going to

be that easy. Alerted by my actions, the two females

rushed up on either side of me. They threw a fire sticks and at the dark shape. I lunged forward, barking and gnashing my teeth. There, in the glare of the flames, I saw her. It was only for an instant. Strangely, I knew what this animal was. I had seen them on the moving wall with the loud sounds. "It's a wolf" Da Da would laugh, "it's only on TV!". I never understand why June and he, found this so funny. Ignoring them, I would rush towards the moving wall to the wolf go away. The wolf in front of me now did the same. With

a flash of grey fur and large sharp pointy teeth, she

had slipped back into the darkness. It was like she

had never been there.

When the light slowly came again my longing for

the return of my pack faded with the darkness. I faced

a need of greater importance. Until lately going

without food was a rare thing in my life. I had it all,

lake, woods, a warm house to live in.

It hadn't started of that way. I was having memories now of an earlier time. I was English to begin with, or at least the people who had owned the puppy mill I came from were. I did know my mother for a sort time there. I miss my mother. My brothers and I had been sent to a pet store. There were a lot of nice people that came to see us and the other puppies there. My brothers were a bit larger. I think that's why they went away first. One day my master came and played with me. He liked to play rough, and we tussled about for a time. I liked the way we played with each other. When we left there together I remember it was very cold outdoors. There was a great storm that day, but my new owner picked me up and put me inside his big coat to keep me warm. I knew then he would always protect me. He took me home to June and they became my new family. I took quite a while for me to train them. Once they had provided me some proper chew toys, in order to save their slippers, things worked out. In the end I even got to sleep on their bed. I had insisted on that. I delighted in rolling around on the clean white linen sheets, placing my scent on them. Da Da would bark about it, but then, June would let me do anything I wanted. I miss June.

Like any dog, I was constantly hungry, I was born that way, but if I played it right there was always food to get. Sometimes I even got a treat called smoked oysters and little dark fish eggs on a tiny crunchy biscuit. Now I'd give my left nut for a bowl of kibble. Not eating here was the new norm and that wasn't going to work out. I was on my own and unless I wanted to be someone's fur bedcover I was going to have to find my own food.

I had surveyed the area close to my den when I first arrived here. There was, I remembered, a source of fast food in the rocks just above.

The plan was to explore in a limited range and to avoid any animal more significant than myself. A big moo cow once tried to head butt me through a wooden fence. You don't forget something like that. Since I got here, I have had it on with a very angry teddy bear, and the giant pig with a sharp point on its face. It seemed a good idea to stay close, just in case I had to make run for it.

I began my hunt, moving upwards beyond where no grass was under my toes. The light here was strong and warm. I found my prey sunning itself on a flat rock. It's how they get warm I think. When he flicked his head towards me, I leaped at him. The lizard disappeared into the rocks. This same scenario played out a number of times, so I began again with a different tactic.

I ran madly along the rocks, jumping and biting at anything that moved. There were a lot these things. I might get lucky. When my jaws crushed the head of one big slow lizard, I shook him like my chew toy. When I was sure he wasn't moving anymore, I dropped him at his feet.

The lizard was my first kill. I had caught small lizards on my walk, but June would always make me spit them out. Once, when I slipped my leash, I had run down a bun bun, but then I didn't know how to play with him without hurting him. Da Da took my collar, and the bun bun ran away and hid in the bushes.

I raced back to the big den to proudly dropped my prize at the feet of the two females. They were so happy they gave me a dried piece of meat to chew on, then they threw the fat lizard onto the fire. This seemed to be a fair trade, due to the fact I hated the taste of lizard. There was always a bad taste on my tongue after I held one in my mouth. I went back to catch a bigger lizard.

I found one sliding through the grass. It was a very long lizard, and I didn't seem to have any feet. I had seen little ones like this in our garden. "Snake!" June would cry out. Then she would run away. That snake looked more like a tiny worm compared to this one. Thinking, if June was afraid of these things, I had best leave it well enough alone, when It turned its head and locked its eyes on me. For a moment, I couldn't seem to breathe. It rose its big head, flicking its forked

tongue between fangs.

 It slid forward, spinning and coiled its thick body.

With a loud hiss, It's head shot straight into my face.

I flinched sideways. The snake's open fangs closed

onto me, tearing a wad of matted fur from my chest.

Turning my head, I brought my jaws down on his neck

with the force of a baby pit bull.

Dropped the big snake on the floor, I sat proudly back, waiting for the women's approval. I wagged my tail happily. I was a very good doggy. Again, they were delighted with my gift, then things went sideways, or at least the snake did. Maybe, I should have made sure it wasn't moving before I gave it to them? The snake was whirling about, trying to bite everyone. The women, like June, began screaming. Uma started hitting at it with her big stick. This party came to a sudden end when Lucy mashed its head into the floor with a massive rock.

We ate the snake for dinner that night. It came off as being a lot like chicken. June and I loved chicken night. I remember Da Da coming home with hot chicken in shiny bag. We would all sit in the garden and eat. This was like that, only it was Lucy and Uma, and we were sitting in a hole. We ate a lot of snake that night.

It had been a long day. I laid down by the warmth of the fire and closed my eyes. Somewhere in the far distance, a lone wolf howled.

My mind was troubled, and I could find little peace, even in my rest. When at last I dreamed, I dreamed of the snake, slithering towards me in the darkness. It coiled about me, crushing me with its great weight. I couldn't breathe. The snake suddenly disappeared, dragged off by the great she-wolf. They fought, snake and wolf, entwined in a battle of who would devourer the other. She killed the snake, rending it flesh, tearing it into bloodied pieces that fell wriggling to the floor. For a moment, it looked as if the snake had come to its end, but then the pieces grew back into more snakes. The she-wolf continued to destroy them.

In the end, they were too many for her. She

disappeared beneath a swirling mass of biting

serpents.

"Prince, you're having a bad dream." I heard June

say "I need you to wake up."

I raised my head, staring into the silent blackness.

Glad the dream was over. The voice came again.

"Come boy, come, Prince,' June said, "come to me."

I got up onto my feet. The two women were still sound asleep. They didn't seem to have heard the voice. There was a brief glitter of light, appearing from where the big hole went down into the ground below.

There seemed to be no end of snacks down here. A big fat mouse with a long tail scurried past to hide itself from me. Had I been hungry, I would have made short work of him. I made a mental note in my head to hunt some of them. For right now, anything that could make a meal out of me was off my list.

I was following the sounds coming from the little car that Da Da had left parked in the small hole. June was calling to me, telling me to come to her, or least I think it was June. The glitter of light came again.

Forming into a tiny ball, it flittered through the narrow opening.

The moment I got up on the car seat, it closed in around me. I wondered if we were going to the dog park, or maybe even the market. The many voices grew louder. They said to stay calm, be a good dog and not to be afraid. It would all be over soon. The car began to shake and hum. A sudden green light blared, blinding me. Howled in terror, I clawed and jumping at the small windows. It felt like I was moving faster and faster. It was as if every part of me was coming apart.

I awoke lying in the car seat. Save for a low hum coming from the little car everything was silent. Yawning repeatedly, I got to my feet and shook off what felt like a long sleep.

I had expanded my hunting range. I was running through the snow above where the trees were. When we had snow like this at home, Da Da and I, would go for long walks. I loved the snow. It was so cool and wet on my hot tongue. It was very cold here, but my heavy coat protected me. There were many tracks. Some of them fresh. I sniffed then chewed some tiny pellet I came across. Bun bun, I said to myself. After a while, the tracks I was following, came to a sudden end. My nose told me the animal was still right here, but I couldn't see him. I could hear him breathing shallowly, calming his tiny beating heart beneath the snow.

Leaping up into the air I pounced, snapping my jaws. The bun bun, as pure white as the snow, flew up to hop away from me. Bounding after him, I continued in relentless pursuit. Once again I drove him from cover. This time I caught him as he sprung in the air. He gave a sharp squeak as my jaws thoroughly crushed his head.

Carrying my kill, I was on my way back when I came across her tracks. Although they were not fresh, I learned a great deal from the traces of her urine. She was lactating, a mother perhaps. Blood trace showed pink in the white snow from her passing. I knew to choose to follow the she-wolfs tracks, would bring me right to her. It meant an encounter with an extremely dangerous, and likely wounded animal.

I found her body lying in a shallow den she had made at the tree line. She barely lifted her head at my approach. Her life was ending, Unable to rise to her feet, even to defend herself. I went down in the snow, showing submission that I had no intent to harm her.

Her large eyes studied me intently for a while, trying to understand what kind of animal I was. Everything about me was strange to her.

The small pups beside her nuzzled at her side, stealing what little warmth she had left. I came to her and placed the bun bun in front of her. She was starving. If she didn't eat now, they wouldn't last the night.

It wasn't an easy relationship to build. I bought her something to eat each day. Little by little she began to regain her strength. Her wounds healed slowly. She had been bitten by her own kind. Driven from her pack for daring to mate with a wandering male. Only the alpha male and his omega female had the right to breed. Her punishment had been banishment.

The trust between us continued to grow. I licked her wounds for her, helping them heal faster. When she was stronger, we would play together, bounding through the snow. Her cubs grew larger and stronger with each visit. One day, she took me forcefully by the back of my neck. Lifted me up, she dragged me to lie next to them. They gathered about me like a warm blanket. Caring for her pups came naturally for me. Playing with them was pure joy. If they got out of line, I would give them a nip or a swat with my paw. Sometimes I would lift them, dragging them back, as my mother and their mother had me. I miss my mother.

After a while, when I had gained her trust, the she-wolf would go out on her own, to hunt for food.

One night, just before the darkness came, and I was alone with her pups, we received a visit from a large male wolf. He stood watching us from a distance for a time, then moved off.

I was to return one last time. The light was strong and the day was warm. The pups were old enough now and were playing, exploring beyond the safety of their den. I lay next to their mother, watching over them.

The she-wolf pricked up her ears, then sprung to her feet. There was a sound like someone laughing or crying on the wind. They came swiftly with little warning. These animals were not dogs, nor were they wolfs.

Their ragged fur was spotted, and their ears and tail were short. Hooting and snarling, they rushed in on us, intent on snatching up one of the cubs. There were so many. The she-wolf spun, faced down three of them, growling and gnashing her teeth. Two of the

attackers opened their sharp, ragged teeth, ready to
divide one of the pups between them.

My heart was pounding widely. I felt like I was
burning up from the inside. I flew high up into the air.
An unbearable pain was racing through my flesh. I felt
myself becoming suddenly larger, stronger. I fell on
my attackers, tearing into them. My now massing jaws
came down on one, crushing its skull like the bun bun.
It exploded in my mouth in a wash of brains and blood.

The she-wolf tore the throat out of her assailant then shouldered another to the ground. She fell on him. After tearing off his balls, she proceeded to rip open his insides. The remaining two remaining attackers turned and fled. I charged after them, pounding through the snow. At the point that I overtook them, they turned to fight. Circling me, they slashed at me with their ragged teeth. I caught one in mid-air, ripping out his throat in a bright spray of blood. The other just seemed to come apart in strips and pieces of bloodied meat. I stood looking over their dismembered bodies. My giant shadow stretched out before me over the pink snow. Somehow, I was not in real body anymore. The tracks I had made with my enormous paws, were larger than any canine that I have ever encountered. I returned to the she-wolf. Neither she, nor her cubs, had been harmed. The she-wolf was looking up at me, putting herself between her cubs and me. She began to growl. What she saw, this thing I had become, terrified her. If she attacked, I wouldn't be able to stop myself. I would kill them all. The confusion I felt, was too much. Turning, with my tail between my legs, I ran from her. I could feel her behind me, nipping at my heals. She was driving me off.

By the time I had left the snow line and reached the safety of my pack, the burning and pain had gone from me. I was slowly becoming myself again.

It wasn't hard for Lucy to see something was wrong with me. The fact that I returned entirely covered in blood was a clear hint that something horrendous had happened to me. We lay together by the fire, as she softly stroked my head. I was no longer a good dog. I had become terror itself — the living flesh of my own nightmares.

The two women kept me close for a few days.

When at last I could summon the courage, I went to find the den in the hill. I found it empty.

One night I heard the call of the she-wolf, only at a greater distance. Another voice joined in with hers, perhaps the lone male that I had seen, who had been searching for a mate.

Chapter 8 - STAR CHILD

Our journey homeward, following the great hunt, was to be an arduous one, due to the massive amount of meat we now had to transport back with us. Thankfully two of the men from the aggressive tribe we had encountered (both barely in their teens) had decided to join in with us. Honestly, I think they thought they would be better off with us. In any case, where ever they had come from, they had no interest in returning there. I started calling them John and Ringo, due to their mop-like hair. Together we constructed sledges, which consisting of two poles and some hide. Loaded with our bounty and dragging them behind us, we started homeward. At the first stream, we encountered the teenagers washing the war paint off their faces. In the days ahead we got to know them a lot better. They had the same mother but different fathers, so were half-siblings. Their parents had been killed by the large fierce man the great mammoth had put an end to.

We returned on the eve of the third day. Lucy and Uma had been worried sick because we had been gone so long. Uma gathered up her boys scolding them and hugging them at the same time. Lucy showered Bob with kisses then took him away where they could sit quietly and talk. It appeared she had something important to say to him. Prince just really wanted to know about the half ton of meat we just dragged in. He went running from one person to another, wagging his tail, desperately trying to get everyone's attention.

We had returned as successful hunters to provide food for our people, and all were relieved that we were safe and whole. There were also two young and strong men for us to welcome into our tribe. There was much to celebrate, and tonight there was to be a great feast to give thanks. Uma had set up racks near the cave entrance in order to begin the process of drying the meat. She smiled, humming to herself as she worked. That is the way I will always remember her.

Our meal that night was more about quantity. You could eat until you popped and I think Ringo came close to doing just that. He laid with his head in his brother's lap groaning loudly. If I could have translated his words it would be, "Why did you let me eat so much?" I chose to roast my steak in the fire much to Uma disapproval. A hunter must always consume what he has killed. It is his way of honoring the life he has taken. I was taking the mammoth into myself. His flesh into my flesh, making him a part of me.

Later after dinner Bob, Lucy, and I sat by the fire looking up at stars. Everyone else, either from overeating exhaustion or both, was pretty much unconscious. It was a quiet peaceful moment and I was drawn to thinking about my life before. I was happy here, and I had come to love these people, but I missed June. She was everything to me. Lucy reached up to the celestial brilliance of the night sky.

"Aha!" she whispered.

Yes, all was indeed beautiful, I agreed. She took my hand, guiding it and placed it on her middle so that I could feel the life growing there. I expressed my great happiness for them. She and Bob were with child. a child that was a direct link to my own existence. I knew I would have to leave them soon, and I knew just how much I would miss them.

Bob rose to his feet and pointed his finger into the heavens. He looked at me as if I might have an answer. Halley's, if it was indeed Halley's, appeared much closer now, so close that its tail seemed to stretch across the sky.

"Aha!?" he asked. He pointed his finger at me. It was as if he thought that I and the comet were connected somehow.

That night, I had a most disturbing dream.

Chapter 9 - FISH STORY

The days that followed were pleasant. There was more than enough to eat and with the help of John and Ringo, there was also an abundance of firewood. We played games to pass the time using rock, sticks, shells, or whatever was at hand. John was particularly good at these, mostly because he thought up most of them. When he lost he took it good-naturedly, then, went about thinking up some new rules. John won a lot of games. Ironically, Ringo had carved out a flute and stretched a skin over a hollow log to make a passible drum. He was starting up a band. Our time of leisure soon gave way to boredom and in a few days Bob came up with a whole new adventure to tempt us with. We were to go fishing he said, giving me a conspiratorial wink. It was just to be us, men. Uma was pleased because she didn't want her boys to be out of her sight. She made the excuse that there was still some work to do and that she would need their help. We packed up the night before so as to get an early start in the morning. I asked why we were taking so much of our meat with us and Bob just shrugged. We were going to need it and that we would be gone for a few days is the best I could get out of him.

The next morning, we said our goodbyes. Bob had to pry Lucy off of him as we left. Prince had made up his mind to come with us. He used his sad eyes on me and I didn't have the heart to refuse him. A fishing trip seemed safe enough. The weather was fair and we made good time. On the second day, we reached a collection of huts edging a marsh, near a wide river. Bob was known to these people and we were well received. The meat that we had brought was to be traded for a goodly assortment of fish and wild foul. Our tribe had much we could learn from them. They were clever hunters, using traps and spears to attain a diverse and reliable food supply. What they couldn't eat, they traded with others for what they needed. Someday, I could see a great city evolving from this place.

Prince made himself instantly popular with the children, playing his version of fetch. Throw something (in this case a strip of hide), and he would dash off dutifully. Getting him to return what you threw, was where all this breaks down. It was his now and in no way were you getting it back. I blame myself. I had never made any serious effort to dog train him. Prince, having his own mind for some reason always seemed more important to me than his obedience. I could tell him to sit, but it was up to him if he wanted to or not. Gangs of little ones raced after him, trying to snatch the bit of hide from his jaws. Thus, the game he played was more like keep away, ending in an intense battle of tug of war.

We ate well around their fire that night, sharing many stories. I heard my name, mentioned in praise, many times. If Bob was alive in the future, he could have got a job as someone's press secretary. Word of my exploits had already spread here, and this tribe was honored to have me in their presence. Apparently, the man who I had been wrongfully accredited for killing, had been much feared by these people. In their mind, they owed me a great debt. So much so that by the evening's end, the elders presented me with not one, but three of their most desirable young women. This gift put me in a very difficult position. To decline, would be a clear and direct insult. I counted forty spears around us. Injuring their pride by saying your daughters are all ugly was not in our best interest. On the other hand, should I choose to accept, I would then be burdened with an unrelenting sense of nagging guilt. Autism means having a lot of baggage of what you did right or wrong. You get to carry that around through your life.

I thought of all the unsuccessful efforts I would have to undertake in lying to my wife. Guilt and lying are things most people with autism have a great deal of trouble carrying off. We really suck at it. Keeping secrets from someone you care about is even harder. Often, unless you have considerable skill, the person you're making up stories for can see right through you. For my experience, one lie leads to others you have to create in order to cover up for the first one. Soon everything in your whole life becomes a lie. I didn't need any more baggage. I had enough already.

That said, I'd be lying here if I said I didn't desire these beautiful girls, so enticingly lit, dancing beneath the moonlight. Thank god there wasn't a hot tub around, or honestly, I'm sure I would have caved.

One of the young women ceremonially placed an offering of drink in my hands and bid me to put it to my lips. There was a general hush. I could feel everyone's eyes on me. I sipped it down in a single gulp. It was as harsh as it was sweet. I felt it trickle down my throat like sweet poison. When the aftertaste kicked in, I was already on my knees. Everything was spinning. Fighting to remain conscious, my mind kept drifting to random visions. "Why was June dancing on a clamshell in a short dress, with all the tribe around her?" I tried to focus, making the vision of my wife go away. I knew these people had given me drugs, but somehow the effects let me see the truth, and the truth was, I was lonely. June's voice was there for me to talk to but, it wasn't her. It wasn't real. My wife was, I hoped, still in Paris with me from the future, having the time of her life, a joy I had to remind myself that I was destined to share with her someday. I have lived my life partly as an artist, and I had always wanted us to see the Louvre together. It felt somehow wrong for me to be jealous of myself, but the truth was, I was. The vision of me knocking on their hotel door and punching me in the nose kept coming into my thoughts.

I took a long deep breath and tried to collect myself to the point I could speak. I asked Bob to translate, that "I had someone who had already claimed me, but that the two handsome and worthy men in our company were both looking for mates." The elders, having considered this a wise decision, clapped me on the shoulders while showing me all of their teeth. It suddenly occurred to me, that I could have simply said no, and maybe that would have been alright. From the wide grins on my two young friends faces, I felt I had played this well. John, who was smothered in girls, gave me a thumbs up. Bob, who I really was seeing as a bear at that moment, came over to me and gave me his hug.

"Good fishing, ha, Furuck?" He shouted.

"I can see colors," I shouted back at him. I waved my fingers in front of my face. "look, trails!"

They say if you remember Woodstock then you weren't really there. From this point on, things get even more weird. Rational thought was quickly slipping away. All the children and the older members of the tribe had found their beds by now. The tribe got into full party mode. I was a hippie at a beach party. Ringo was chewing on some kind of tree bark. One of the women placed a fragrant flower under my noise, then jammed it into my mouth. As they said in the 60's "You got to know how to mix your drugs man." Well, I was mixing drugs and didn't have a clue what was inside me. Someone tapped me on the back. The old man with a toad in his hand offered me a lick. I declined, having still enough sense to know I was already well beyond Woodstock. The old man shrugged happily and went away sucking on his toad.

With Ringo leading the band, we danced on into the wee hours of the morning. Just when this was slowing down, Bob came to me holding a torch, forcing me and the others to come with him. Apparently, this party was just getting started.

In an opening in the hill above warm water steamed from the rock to collect in shallow pools. A lot of the youthful members of the tripe were here already, soaking in the warm water or taking part in the wild sex orgies that were erupting about me. I was too busy to notice. My insides were having an adverse reaction to the drugs I had consumed. I spent a lot of time leaning over a bush, with my finger down my throat, retching my guts out.

When I returned to join the others in the hot pool, I was I found myself in a better state of both mind and body. Drugs are bad, I tried to remind myself, but the delightful buzz I had on, said otherwise.

In the future, in a time when I had once lived, we were fighting a losing battle against drugs. People were dying. Almost everyone knew someone that had. Some were old; others were barely in their teens. The drugs couldn't distinguish whether they were rich or poor. It didn't discriminate. It killed them just the same. Often, the people that made and sold the drugs had more money than a small nation. Some of these drugs in question, chiefly the opiates, came right from pharmaceutical corporations, who, when you think about it, are the largest drug pushers in our world.

Prince swam past, enjoying the warm water. The mud and filth that fell off him was enough to start a small grow op. I saw the girl face down in the water. I grape her hair and pulled her up. She smiled, took a deep breath, and sunk down into the water to engulf me. This was making it hard to ignore the massive tribal cluster fuck that was happening on all sides of me, I lay back, staring up at the planet killer hovering over our heads. Never had I seen an image of a comet so close to the proximity to the earth. June and I, using the visor, had studied its progress, and had come to the conclusion that it had already just squeaked by earth's gravitational field, and was now on its way towards the sun. Although comets advertise themselves impressively, in truth they are disappointingly insubstantial. Only the largest of them, like this one, contained enough mass to be a threat.

It was the tail we were likely to pass through that had me concerned. A comet's tail contains rocks and ice and gas. Should any fragmented pieces, caught by earth's gravitation, fall into our atmosphere, we could take a hit.

The sheer numbers of meteorites now silently

streaking through the sky, had gained some attention.

Those members of the tribe, who were not fucking,

were watching it like it was a fireworks display. Every

once I a while there would be an, oooh or an ah, as a brighter object came down and then snuffed out. None of these would ever reach the ground, burning up in the last one hundred kilometers. The night lit up for a second. Everyone looked up the see what looked like a dozen stars shoot downwards, hurtling towards us. These bigger pieces were only the harbingers of a more significant threat.

"Here it comes," I said to myself. I had seen this moment in my dreams, over and over. "How," I asked myself "how I could know this?"

Night was instantly transformed into day. I barely had time to come to my feet.

The rock broke through the atmosphere in blue

flames. Shielding our eyes, we watched it tear

overhead. Just like in my dreams, it fell from the

heavens, like an avenging angel. With every second, it

traveled future and further, away from us. A bluish

trail of burning dust and gas chased after it. No one

made a sound. There wasn't time. Just when the

deafening roar of its passing reached us, the part of the rock that hadn't burned up, struck beyond the distant hills. A flash, white-hot, came first, so bright I could see the bones of the people in front of me, then went to a powerful shock wave.

The blast knocked me and everyone else to the ground. A great deal of the forest around us was instantly flattened. The land itself rose up. Throwing us into the air, we fell back onto a wounded earth. Its spine broken by a giant. The ground wouldn't settle, shaking, and writhing under us. It had to deal with its pain.

All the air shot forward, rushing back toward the blast, taking it from our lunges. Bodies around me, flew from the rocks, to fall to their peril below. It was like I was breathing in a vacuum.

Those who could struggled to get to their feet. The glow from behind the mountain came as a false dawn. Everything out there was on fire. A boiling mushroom cloud, growing ever larger, was jetting up into a violent sky. Lightning ripped through it like serpents, adding to its menace. My eyes traveled to where the village has stood.

Few of the rude huts had survived. The rest were chaff in the wind. Bodies were lying everywhere. They looked as if they had been flung there, all of them facing away from the blast. Some among them were moving. One small child was walking, a toddler, screaming for its mother. I collected everyone I could and headed down to search for survivors.

We had placed the dead in rows. I counted eighteen, which included two that had fallen from the hill above. Thankfully, there were no children amongst them. Due to all the noise, we had been making the night before, all of them had been sleeping in the larger huts, that had survived the blast. The tribe's eldest woman, who looked a lot like my mother, had been left in charge of them, was cuddling them, trying to give them comfort. Some of their parents that lay among the dead. I had taught first aid when I was young, and I put that knowledge to good use. The old man, (that had offered me the toad), had been impaled by a sharp fragment of wood. There was red foam gurgling from a small hole in his chest. I passed him over to help someone I might save. The bank of the river had sheltered many. Those huts close to the water's edge had got the worst of it. That's where most of the bodies were. There were a few deep cuts that needed attention, but most of the survivors had come off with having the wind knocked out of them. There were a lot of bruises and scratches.

I was thinking, that we had got off lucky when the fish fell from the sky. Along with snow like ash and hail, they pelted down onto us, flipping and flopping on the ground. I ran to the river's bank to see the water pulling rapidly away from the shore. In seconds the once mighty river was reduced to a stream. People were just standing there, watching it happen, trying to understand this. Prince gave me a look, then raced towards higher ground.

"Run, everyone run!" I shouted, waving my arms. "Bob, we have to make them go up there!" I pointed to the hills. "Now!"

These people were terrified already. My fear caused an instant panic. Everyone began running.

You could hear it before you could see it. From this distance it looked like a dark grey line at the mouth of the river, rushing swiftly towards us. There in its path, frozen with terror, a speck on the wet sand, stood the little girl that had been crying for its mother. I ran towards her, ripping up the ground under my feet. The horizon had turned into a dark thundering wall of water. It swelled up higher and higher. Snatching up the toddler, I turned back.

I could feel the monster growing behind me, but I couldn't take the chance to look back. Every second counted. The wave curled and then collapsed surging around me. Reaching the bottom of the embankment I hurled myself up into the air, grasping for a handhold in the rocks above me. The water crashed after me, trying to pull me back down. I held on, refusing to let it take me. Suddenly, Bob was there, taking the child from me. He reached out for my hand. The old woman scream rose above the tempest. I looked back to see her flailing about in the surge, only meters from me.

"No Furuck!" Bob warned.

The woman disappeared, sucked down beneath the water. I couldn't do it. Letting go of Bob's hand, I threw myself back, diving into the water. It devoured me. I found myself spinning round and round, caught by the waves power. It wanted me dead. For a fleeting second, I saw the old woman. She was almost within reach. I struck out with powerful strokes and took her by the hair. A wild surge drove us forward. I took advantage of it, moving with its momentum. Using every once of my remaining strength, I heaved the woman up onto rocks. Bob and the villagers were there, to pull both of us to safety.

The next few days were beyond miserable. We built lean-tos in the forest beyond the river's bank for shelter. The steady fall of ash and hail made making a fire nearly impossible. The old woman I had saved died of exposure sometime in the night. Although there was plenty of fish lying around, thankfully we still had the food we had brought with us. The wind favored us, holding back the fire and smoke. Beyond the distant mountains, the flames glowed menacingly but appeared to be moving away from us.

I got very little sleep. When I did, I kept having the same dream. I saw the piece of the comet falling, reliving it over and over. "There had to be a reason for that?" I thought. Next time the dream came, it was different. I could see it more clearly. The rock had become a giant saucer-like disk. Burning white blue, it hurtled towards the earth. Parts of it were tearing off as if to escape from a falling star. I kept hearing a roaring sound, like some wounded beast. It rapidly became a scream. At first, I thought it was the dying mammoth, then I realized, it was my wife. June was screaming out in terror. She was on that ship.

When the ship struck the earth, it detonated,

destroying everything in a blaring white light.

That morning the sun found its way through the clouds. The remaining elders and I looked down onto what little remained of their village. The waters had receded enough to again make out the outline of the shore. All the bodies were gone, washed away like everything else. The elders spoke among themselves for a moment, then gathering their people, made their way down.

They built until it was too dark to see. John had made it understood that the new huts were to be stronger and larger. These he had made into a protective circle, positioned higher on the embankment. Worker together, he and his brother Ringo, turned out to quite the builders. Unbeknownst to them, was they had already selected by the two of the young women, aiding them.

"At least some good, might come out of all this." I thought.

That night, we sat around our fire. Its light gave us warmth and hope. Having done as much good as we could, Bob and I decided to leave in the morning. Our return was long overdue, and our own people would be worried for us.

In the morning we said our goodbyes. We left with two young brides for our friends, and enough food to get us home.

We stopped on the hillside, viewing the group of huts, and the people who inhabited them. Many were already going about with the work of their day. Their children ran about, playing in the warm sunshine. The wide river, that had sustained them, again flowed past, making its way towards the sea. It was a place of great beauty that had been scarred by great tragedy, and yet these people would carry on. They would be the ancestors on nations. "Could this be Paris?" I wondered to myself. With Prince at my heels, I led my people back into the waiting forest.

Chapter 10 - THROUGH A DARK MIRROR

With each step on our journey homeward, we left the signs of the devastation further behind us. Soon we were moving through green forest, untouched by the effects of the impact. By late noon, with the sun at our backs, our mood began to lighten.

With the addition of the two young women, we had become a stronger tribe. For us, their presence gave us hope for the future. John and Ringo, looked like they had been struck by lightning. Both the power of lust and love had hit them at the same time. The boys couldn't take their eyes off of them. The girls, for their part, let them catch their eyes from time to time. Who got to be with who was the game being played. By experience, I have always found these things have a way of working out in the end. Although, the humor in this interaction, was the girls letting the boys think the decision was theirs to make. I gave the girls names I could pronounce. In the end, it came down to my wacky autistic humor, so they got to be Yoko and Ono.

On the second day, as the way home became more and more familiar, our strides quickened. In the far distance, the fires beyond the mountains raged on. Clouds of choking smoke filled the horizon. By midday, the direction of the wind began to change. It came like a warning. Whatever was happening out there, it was now clearly coming our way.

Our luck had run out. The intensity of the wind grew stronger with each passing moment. A threatening darkness grew ever closer. It became imperative that we return before nightfall. Our survival depended on it. The harsh wind gathered strength, bringing with it a biting cold. The sky darkened, all but blotting out the sun. We pressed on, racing against the advance of some storm. Bolts of lightning ripped into the earth, setting the forest behind us on fire. We needed to find shelter, and we needed to see it soon. Driving snow mixed with ash, began to fall, covered the landscape.

All breathed a sigh of relief when, at last, the entrance of our cave appeared in the hills above. The month of the cave seemed to be dark and forbidding as if waiting ominously for someone to enter it. There was no discernable glow from our fire, nor was there any sign of moment or life. Bob gripped my shoulder. I saw the fear rising in his face. Uma would never have let our fires go out. Dropping everything we were carrying, we ran.

The storm came against us with all its fury. Falling and stumbling through the blinding snow, we fought to reach the caves entrance. Prince ran on ahead of us, barking. The storm took him from our sight, as a sheet of white, swept him into the darkness.

All the fires appeared to have gone cold and dead. The racks that had once held our drying meat, lay shattered about the cave's opening. There was no sign of Prince. John blew on some coals from one of the fires, bringing a torch to life. Centered on the floor, was a large pool of blood. Remnants of what had once been a human body lay scattered about. The rest had been eaten. The light of the torch rested on a woman's severed hand, locked in a death grip, still clutching the handle of a heavy club. Barely a meter away, was the shattered tip of a long yellow tooth. Uma, had at least put up a fight. The enormous footprints, outlined in her blood were unmistakable.

"Katt." Bob said, making the curved two finger sign for a saber tooth.

More light came as the girls quickly resurrected our fire. It was an instinct for them. A fire provided warmth light and most importantly protection, and we desperately needed that right now. There were many tracks. It was impossible for us to tell how many animals had made them. Bob was the first to hear it. Somewhere far below us in the furthest reaches of the cave a small dog was barking. Prince was going to take them on by himself. Whatever he had found down there had turned on him. A powerful roar echoed towards us shaking the cave. We could hear Prince bravely snarled back. A sudden painful yelp followed, then nothing. The silence held, seemingly going on forever. I could feel my heart beating in my chest. The scream when it came was long, piercing the darkness in it terror and despair. Somewhere down there, Lucy was alive.

Slither (Prince's POV)

The animals that had eaten the old woman had gone deep into the ground. The small ones of my pack and my Lucy had run from them. If they were still alive, they wouldn't be for much longer.

The smell of cats was everywhere. I hated cats. Fluffy, a yellow tom, had scarred my nose when I found it hiding in a bush, and that was when I was being friendly. If we ever got home again, I made up my mind, that cat was going to pay. By the urine and tracks I had encountered, I got the idea these cats, like everything else here, were on the large size. Unless I became the other thing, and I had no idea how to do that, I wouldn't stand a chance against even one of them.

I ran down into the hole that went deep into the ground, searching for my alpha. Her scent led me deeper. Deeper into the ground than I had ever gone before. Two cats, seeing me streak past, gave chase. A slash from one of their claws, raking a crossed my flank, sent me spinning. Ignoring the pain, I ran on, leaving them far behind. For some unexplained reason, they had decided to stop chasing me. I could hear my alpha screaming. Lucy was close now.

I sniffed at the giant tracks of the beast that following in her footsteps. There was something else down here. Something even the big cats were afraid of. I hadn't forgotten his smell. You don't forget something like that. He too, had been driven inside by the storm. The giant cave bear had returned to reclaim his home, and he was looking to avenge the loss of his eye.

I welcomed it when the pain came again. It was like every part of me had turned to fire. Falling onto the ground I writhed in indescribable agony. I was becoming again. My body was breaking apart, forming again into some new monstrous mutation. My fur had hardened into scales.

I hunted Lucy by the vibrations I now sensed around me. She was trapped, on the other side of a narrow bridge of stone. The path she had taken spanned a great and endless chasm. One that fell on seemingly forever. Armed with a torch, and her killing spear, Lucy had turned in a last futile attempt to fight for her life. Mindful of the flaming torch, the bear moved towards her across the expanse. I could taste his smell on my tongue. He raised himself, brandishing his massive claws and teeth.

Silently, my new body slid a crossed the bridge. Unaware of my presence, the bear rushed toward his prey. I shot forward. Overtaking him, I whirled about him, quickly coiling my flesh about his massive girth, squeezing his breath and his life from him. Frantically, his claws ripped into me, rending my scales into ragged tatters. I felt the blood leaving my body. His jaws opened wide, ready to tear into me. It was then that he made the mistake of looking in my eyes. I could feel his heart stop in sudden terror. It was all the time I needed. I hissed, spraying my hot venom straight into his face. The mighty bear burst into flames. Howling madly, he staggering blindly back, beyond the edge of the stone path.

Entwined in a deadly embrace, we fell together, hurtle ling down like a dying ember into the yawning darkness. I felt the air rushing past me. Uncoiling my body, I fought to free myself. I felt something rip out from my back, tearing through my flesh. The fall went on forever, but for some reason, this thing I had become, never reached the bottom.

Through a dark mirror (continued)

We stayed together in a tight group relying on our spears and our strength in numbers. Each had a torch to light the way down. The plan was not for anyone else to die. We walked silently in order to listen for our enemy. The cats could see us in the dark, and they could smell us. They knew we were here and they were waiting. If we could make it as far as my hidden cave I could change that. Once I had my suit I was going to personally kill every one of these fucking monsters.

We were halfway there when they sprang on to us. Ringo died in the first second, his body dismembered in the air. One of the saber-tooth females fell beneath the wall of our spears. The dark shadows around us disappeared back into the darkness. Occasionally, we could see their eyes reflecting at the edge of the light from our torches. We had traded one for one, and our enemy had become wary.

Ahead, a small voice called out from the blackness. There was an instant retaliated response from the Tigers. John threw his torch giving light in that direction. Another female and her cub were trying to force their way into a tiny opening in the rock. The tip of a spear darted out at them, was all that was keeping them back. John and Bob were there first driving the attackers off. John hurled his javelin after the mother, wounding her in the hindquarters. We found the twins alive, but both had been injured. Ugg has lost a lot of blood from a deep gash on his abdomen while Glugg was missing two of his fingers. Both were suffering from shock. The narrow egress in the rock had been the only thing that had saved them.

I charged John to take them back to the safety of
the fires. We had lost two friends already and I wasn't
about to lose anyone else. Bob and I would go on
alone. John showed me his spear in protest. He was
warrior. His place was with us. I pointed to the
frightened women and children, indicating the many
wounds among them. They would be of little use in a
fight now. The young man nodded that he understood,
reluctantly doing as I had ordered him. He raised his

spear to me this time in salute (I will be back he was saying), then led them back to safety. There was no sense trying to convince Bob to go with them. He wouldn't have gone. Lucy and his unborn child were down here, and he had to find them.

My hidden cave was barely twenty meters. If we could cover that ground, we had a chance. They came at us rushing in from every side. There was no way to tell how many they were.

"Run!" I screamed.

The caves narrow opening was before us when a large male with a broken tooth dropped down from above, blocking our way. I swung my stone axe erasing the rest of his teeth then brought it down splitting his scull. Leaping over his body we gained the safety of the cave. I rushed to arm myself with my suit as Bob guarded the entrance. A soft whimper caused me to look down. Prince had found safety, hiding himself under the time machine. There was a lot blood, but there was no way of telling if all of it was his. This was still the safest place for him right now. I told firmly him to stay and put on my visor. Night vision was instantly engaged. A tactical screen went up showing our positions and an incomplete mapping of the cave. It was a lot bigger than I had thought.

June's voice was direct and professional,

"Estimating six targets remain, consisting of five adult males, also one female, and one juvenile."

"What are our chances, can we take them?" I asked.

"Unlikely" she replied. "Unarmed, you have less than a forty present chance of survival. Additionally, should you die, so will everyone else."

My mind was racing, trying not to go into full panic mode. One thought kept coming back into head. There was only sure way I could win this. I gave Bob the axe and convinced him wait here for me. I would come back and together we would find Lucy.

"Promise me you'll stay here?" I said, then, charged out the opening.

All seven targets on my screen, marked in red, converged on me at once. I could see them surging towards me. Leaping past them, I ran, forcing the cats to pursue me. I had gained a distance from them when I again found the pool of dark water. Locating its greater depth, I dove, submerging into utter darkness; my hood and glasses instantly transforming for the dive downward. For some reason I knew I would be able to breath here.

"How will my air last?" I asked.

June replied that it was unlimited, but that the suit was not authorized beyond a depth of forty-two meters.

"I have located your target at sixty-one meters. It is strongly advised that you abort your attempt." She said coldly.

Dislodging a large rock, I used its weight, letting it pull me down into the abyss. I could see the locating blip centered on my screen. Every second brought me closer to it. The pressure was building up, becoming unbearable. A ringing in my ears made it hard to think. At fifty-one meters the air gave out. I held my last breath, grasping for the shiny object just below me. I took hold of it, dropped the rock, and shot for the surface. When the air returned I was close to blacking out.

June's voice was speaking to me, repeating something over and over, "He's in the water with you. Acquire target, five meters! Acquire target, two meters!"

My screen showed something above me closing fast. Breaking free of the water I spun towards it and fired.

The gun produced no recoil. The round that hit the saber tooth looked like a bolt of electrified thunder. It tore off most of the animal's head. Its burning corpse slipped hissing beneath the water.

Strolled through the cave I began hunting them. It was I who now had the advantage.

"Here, kitty, kitty?" I called, but encountered nothing.

The question became, if they weren't here, where had they gone, and why? I came across the wounded mother and cub first. Their bodies lay strewn on the cave floor. Something very heavy had smashed both their heads in. Apparently Bob hadn't waited for me.

"June locate Lucy and Bob?" I shouted.

My display showed their position in white at one hundred and twenty meters. The five remaining targets, shown in red, were directly in front of them. My friends were walking into a trap. I ran covering the distance so fast at times I felt the ground shaking beneath me.

I came up onto the edge of the battle. Checking my speed to get a clear shot, I razed my gun. Bob and Lucy had their backs together, valiantly welding death against foes on every side. Bob was hurling fire and axe, holding off two large males, at arms reach. Lucy appeared to be ascending demonically upwards, spear pulled back, ready to trust, facing the claws and fangs of another. She had thrown a small pouch toward the fallen torch on the cave floor before her. She screamed out in warning just as the nitrate burst over the flame. My visor darkened for a moment, protecting me from the heat flash. The saber - tooths had been thrown back, blinded and disorientated. I began firing. My first rounds severed one in two. Bright sprays of crimson blood seemed to hang in the air. My second grouping brought down the one closest to Lucy. Bob had beaten the remaining tiger into the cave floor. He didn't stop. When he was sure it was dead enough he dropped the stone axe, then returned to Lucy's side. He took her into his arms, holding her protectively. She clung to him and began to weep uncontrollably. I still see this moment to this day, imprinted there in my autistic memory, forever to be recalled.

None saw the giant shadow leaping down onto them from the darkness, no one but June.

Her voice was screaming, "Acquire target! Acquire target!"

It came down a split second. Had I have acted in anything less than that, Lucy and her child would have died, and I might never have been born. I can never recall how many rounds I fired. Some had cleanly missed, exploding in the walls and ceiling of the cave. The fateful bullet that hit Bob spun him around like a toy. The others drove into the tiger's massive body. The force of the impacts seemed to almost hold it there, suspended it in the air, then, it fell lifeless and burning onto the cave floor. The battle we had fought had been hard won, but our victory had come at great cost. I remember thinking, I had told myself I couldn't change anything, that whatever happens, would always happen. The lesson was I couldn't change time. Despite everything I had done to prevent this moment, in the end, I stood with a gun in my hand, and my friend's broken body lay face down in its own blood. The bullet that I had fired had his name on it right from the very beginning.

Everything shifted strangely, becoming unreal. I staggered backwards as the ground beneath me seemed to sway. A low rumbling grew steadily louder and louder. Walls of choking dust fell, making it hard to see. The cave's ceiling, weakened by the explosions, began to come crashing down. I dodged a large fall of rock that almost fell on top of me. For a brief moment, through the dust, I could see Lucy rocking Bob's body in her arms. His eyes were open and staring into mine. I couldn't tell if he were alive or dead. The cave was collapsing around them and me. My very last sight of them was of John and the girls, dragging them away from the danger. At least that is what I'd like to believe I had seen. A curtain of dust and rock fell between us, taking them from my view. I was seconds away from being buried alive.

"Run!" June was screaming, "For God's sake you have to run!"

I crawled through the entrance of the small cave on my hand and knees. Behind me a large section of the outer cave gave way. It wasn't stopping. I knew that there was only one chance to survive. Prince's body was limp. He didn't appear to be breathing. Gathering him up I jumped into the seat of the time machine, flashed up the controls, and waiting for the large red button to come on. Everything was shaking around me. We had only seconds.

"Take us home June!" I ordered, "Take us back to our time." The red button flickered. "Do it now!"

"I can't!" she was saying, "I'm sorry, I can't!"

The button glowed red. I hammered it with my fist. There was the searing silence, followed by the gut-wrenching descent into nothingness. I remember thinking, is this what it was like when you die. Then, I and Prince were gone.

I woke as if from a long dream. There was a feeling that I should be doing something, that there was some purpose I didn't yet fully understand. It was warm here. The air itself was different. It carried the sent of a musty sweetness tinged with a taste of salt. I took it into my lungs, breathing deeply. Bright sunlight showed through the cracks in the wooden structure that surrounding me. All the windows looked as if they had been boarded up. I had played in places like this when I was a boy. The sweet scent of hay and the chicken pecking at the handles bars of my time machine put it all in place. The events that had just happened to me before were still there in my mind. I tried to put it behind me. Whatever life I had there was gone now. The people I had known had all died countless centuries before. In later years I was to find something in a book of cave drawings attributed to the time and area I might have been. The image was of what looked to be an alien wearing a helmet while pointing a ray gun, standing before a tribe of people.

Prince was breathing, so at least I knew he was still with me. None of the cuts on him appeared to be life-threatening. I made a bed for him on the clay floor and laid him down on it. The barns door was latched with a heavy beam from the inside. I removed it and swung the doors wide. Shielding my eyes, I stepped out into the full brightness of a summer's day. I was on a wide hilltop looking down. Beyond the fertile landscape that surrounded me lay a shining blue sea. Small boats sailed serenely upon its surface, plying its waters for fish. White clouds moved listlessly through an endless sky hovering over an ancient city. I did not need to ask June where I was. The question was when?

- To be continued

OUTRO

This was but the beginning of a long journey. In book two, Vengeful Gods, our heroes will be drawn into both the conflicts of men, and the history they would make. They will undergo many adventures in the face of great peril. Cast upon the wings of an unknown destiny, they must place their trust in their creator, me, to bring them home safe in the finale end. For me, being the creator, carries a very heavy burden. At the end of this story Bob's fate lay in question here, and like you, it haunts me. Did he die there in the darkness, buried alive, gunned down by his best friend, or did he somehow make it? I had a stern word with myself, and it came up as creator, I can pretty much do absolutely anything I like. That said, imagine if your Bob. Notwithstanding the thunder blasts, the whirling cats, and the falling cave bits, you have everything under control. You have in essence, saved the day. Then, just when you're holding your girl in your arms, bang, your freaky friend shoots you a thunderbolt right in the ass cheek. The only reason the shell had not exploded, was because it had decided it was only passing through. Either that or Bob's knotted Neanderthal like ass was so hard the bullet just bounced right off. In any case, it carried on to strike the cave wall. In later years, when his grandchildren called upon him to describe how he had come to having two ass holes, he would say it was when a million bees had stung him on the bum. The pain that had come into his head was like a bright light that took him away, and that when he opened his eyes again, he was laying by the fire. That's all he could remember. He and Lucy's children's children would go on to form the great northern tribes. I feel better, don't you?

I would again truly like to thank you for your continued interest in my books. Each will be available in digital download, a hold in your hand printed copy, or my favorite, in the advanced audiobook format experience. I would ask you to please visit the **ASPERGIAN NATION** website, with whose kind support and guidance, help make the publication of this work possible.

Richad Alan Poe

CHRONICLES OF THE TIME THIEF

an autistic romance

Book Two
VENGEFUL
GODS

featuring an autistic central character

sponsored by - THE ASPERGIAN NATION

Aspergian Nation

Richard Alan Poe

CHRONICLES OF THE TIME THIEF

THE DIVINE

Book three

featuring an autistic central character

Aspergian Nation

THE TRAVELER

Fond remembrance of sweetened kisses,

fading Images of loves adore.

My story told here in lesser glory, that I lived

As you and those who've gone before.

From nothingness came I, born out of

Creation's timeless dust.

A child my eyes did lift, amid jeweled fields

and amberoid shards of rust.

A man I rose in shining seas of azure blue,

to breath in depths of burning desire.

A sensual slave, wilful to my youth,

consumed by passions relentless fire.

Through emerald forests cool and deep I ran.

Beyond the scented glades.

Willingly down the downward path of wisdom,

towards a far golden shore, I made.

Then was my heart won and lost, to one fair

Of beauty, strength, and grace –

Savagely I was felled, by rapture

Of our loves bittersweet embrace.

Unbridled touch a beloved's caress, tender vows,

cherished in promise not to part.

In voice we sang with tearful refrain, this bliss

inside our hearts.

Together we grew to share our lives, to

drink of sorrow, joy, and love.

Into a world often ravaged by anger, we gave

our children onto the wings of doves.

Yet the way to my journey still lay before me,

cast across an infinite plain. Mounted 'pon a shrouded

steed of fate, softly, destiny pulled the reins.

And now as I slowly walk, in the darkened shadow of

twilight's gleam.

Softly does my soul transcend, the eternal

night of ebon dreams.

I was but a weary and lonely traveler, that

rode once a mortal plain,

and long may be the road I journey, ere come I, this

way again.

Richard Alan Poe